Matilda
and
Hans

For Tilly, Eva, and Magnus

First U.S. edition 2013

Library of Congress Cataloging-in-Publication Data is available.
Library of Congress Catalog Card Number pending
ISBN 978-0-7636-6434-3

TWPS 18 17 16 15 14 13 12
10 9 8 7 6 5 4 3 2 1

Printed in Singapore

This book was typeset in Times New Roman.
The illustrations were done in mixed media and watercolor.

Produced by Templar Publishing

TEMPLAR BOOKS

an imprint of Candlewick Press
99 Dover Street
Somerville, Massachusetts 02144

www.candlewick.com

Yokococo

Matilda and Hans

templar books
an imprint of Candlewick Press

There once was a good little cat

named Matilda . . .

and a naughty little cat
named Hans.

They were SO different!

Matilda was quiet . . .

and Hans was loud!

Matilda was always well behaved . . .

and Hans always

misbehaved.

Matilda was thoughtful . . .

and Hans caused

trouble.

One night Hans climbed

the gates of the zoo . . .

took the keys . . .

and set all
the animals free!

Oh, dear!

WANTED

$1,000 REWARD

for information leading to the arrest of
a naughty cat (answers to the name of Hans)

The next day,
Matilda saw a poster
offering a reward for
information about Hans.

So she went to the
police station.

"Excuse me," said Matilda. "I think I know where you could catch Hans tonight."

And she told the policeman where he would be.

That night, the policeman
caught Hans red-handed
right where Matilda
said he would be.

and his mask . . .

Then Hans took off

his hat . . .

and his whiskers.

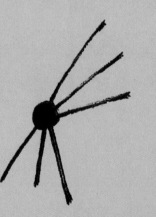

"Can I have the reward now, please?"
Matilda asked very sweetly.

She promised that Hans would be
good from then on.

And Hans was . . .

But not

Matilda!